Virus

Virus

J. E. Stock

Library of Congress Control Number:		2021911510
ISBN:	Hardcover	978-1-6641-7897-7
	Softcover	978-1-6641-7898-4
	eBook	978-1-6641-7896-0

Print information available on the last page.

Rev. date: 06/16/2021

To order additional copies of this book, contact:
Xlibris
844-714-8691
www.Xlibris.com
Orders@Xlibris.com
827753

This book is dedicated to my family, whose patience and understanding made this book possible.

April 1, 2025

Washington DC

D R. MICHAEL GATES, the director of the National Institute of Allergy and Infectious Diseases, is meeting with his supervisor, Dr. Samuel Page, the director of the National Institutes of Health.

"Sam, we need to do gain of function research on influenza viruses."

"Are you crazy? You know how risky that would be? We're still getting back to normal after COVID."

"But influenza could potentially make COVID seem like a walk in the park. We must be prepared, and we can't be unless we study the most dangerous possible mutations."

"If something went wrong, we could wipe out most of the world's population. The answer is no, and it is not open to further discussion."

In a different part of the city, FBI agent Jennifer Barnes is meeting up in a coffee shop with her friend, Secret Service agent James Duncan.

A song ringtone begins playing on another customer's phone. Agent Duncan reacts with a clear sense of frustration, saying, "I think I might go crazy if I hear that song one more time."

"Calm down, you're attracting attention. You don't want to hurt your social credit score."

Another customer pulls out a cell phone and takes a picture of Agent Duncan.

"I know, and I just got on the presidential detail, but I can't help it; I hear that song nonstop on everyone's phone in the White House. I thought I would get a break from it here."

"What do you expect? It was the president's campaign song, and you know how popular he is after just winning in a landslide. Actually, I heard that they are planning to make it the national anthem."

Agent Duncan spits out his coffee. "Oh no, I feel like I'm going to throw up."

Agent Barnes pats him on the back. "I'm sorry. I apologize. You can relax; it was just a bad April Fools' Day joke."

Agent Duncan calms down. "You really know how to push my buttons. Let's change the subject. Have you heard anything recently from any of our college group?"

"No, I've been so busy with work that I haven't had time for anything else."

"I wonder how Bobby is doing. I still feel bad about cutting him off."

"What could we have done? Our career prospects would have been destroyed if we had been connected to him and his crazy conspiracy theories. Susan is the only one who didn't cut him off, and last I heard, she was working as dog walker."

"I just wonder if we're getting carried away with these social credit scores."

A customer at the next table looks over at them.

"Stop it; people are looking at us. I can't afford to have anything happen to my score; I'm in line for a promotion, and I think the scores are being weighted a lot more than the stated 50 percent."

"Okay, okay, calm down." Agent Duncan looks at his watch. "I need to wrap up; we're prepping for the president's trip to China next week."

Dr. Gates paces back and forth in his office and then pulls out his cell phone.

"Hi, it's Mike Gates. Can we follow up on our discussion? As soon as possible. Great, I'm looking forward to it."

About an hour later, the Chinese ambassador enters Dr. Gates's office.

"Thanks for coming over so quickly."

"You are very welcome. You obviously felt the need for urgency."

"Please have a seat."

"Thank you."

"So given the urgency that you noted, is it okay for us to get down to business?"

"Absolutely."

"Okay, as we discussed previously, we will provide the full funding for the gain of function research on influenza viruses at your lab in the underground Yulin Naval Base, and I will have one of our top scientists, Dr. Mark Johnson, lead the effort at the lab. I am bypassing my boss on this one, so we need to maintain tight security. Also, I need your complete assurance that you will close down the entire naval base if anything goes wrong."

"I have consulted the highest levels of our government, and we have an agreement."

"Excellent. Dr. Johnson and I will be part of the group traveling next week with the president on his trip to your country, so we will detour down to Hainan Island to begin the work at your lab. We need you to immediately make all preparations for the research so we can hit the ground running and work 24/7 because I will have to return with the president, and Dr. Johnson will only have a limited amount of time before he will be missed."

"We will be ready."

2

Late April 2025

Secret Bioresearch Lab at Yulin Naval Base in Hainan, China

I T IS PAST midnight, and two agents from the Ministry of State Security are talking in hushed tones. One of them is wearing a biohazard suit and carrying a small medical kit.

The agent in regular clothing says, "Hurry, we need to get out of here before we are noticed. Remember, you are doing this for the Party and you have been bioengineered to be immune to the harmful effects of influenza viruses, but to still be a carrier and remain fully infectious."

While this is occurring, Dr. Johnson watches from a hopefully safe distance.

The man in a biohazard suit opens a door marked "Biosafety Level 4," and after entering, he removes his biohazard suit and other clothing. He enters and walks through a shower area; moves into a changing area, where he puts on a positive-pressure suit; and then walks through the decontamination shower area before finally opening the door to enter the BSL4 lab environment while still carrying the small medical kit.

Once inside, he activates the automated system to select a virus sample. A circular containment device in the interior of the system rotates. He stops the rotation when it reaches a sample labeled "H1N1 maximum HA and PB2 enhancement," and he then uses a robotic arm to retrieve the sample. He opens the medical kit and takes out a syringe, which he uses to extract a portion of the sample. Then he attaches a nasal adaptor to the syringe, removes his protective headgear, and injects the sample into his nasal passageway. After that, he reattaches his headgear and disposes of the syringe and the medical kit.

He then reopens the interior door and exits the lab; when the door is fully closed, he pushes a button labeled "Begin Decontamination Shower." After that shower, he enters the next room, where he removes the positive-pressure suit before entering the next shower. Following that shower, he enters the last room, where he dresses once again in his original biohazard suit before finally opening the last door and rejoining the other agent.

They then depart quickly. As they leave, the one in regular clothing glances in the direction of Dr. Johnson. Dr. Johnson ducks out of sight, hoping that he was not noticed.

After the agents exit, Dr. Johnson enters the BSL4 lab and is shocked when he sees where the automated lab equipment is positioned.

Dr. Johnson returns to his apartment. His body is shaking, and he picks up his cell phone.

"Hello, Mike. Not good. We have a big problem."

There is pounding on the door to Dr. Johnson's apartment.

Someone shouts, "State security. Open immediately."

Dr. Johnson turns toward the door and says into his phone, "The Chinese took the H1N1 maxed out on HA and PB2."

The apartment door is broken open; security agents rush into the apartment and grab Dr. Johnson. One of them says, "You are under arrest." Another one takes the phone out of Johnson's hand and pushes the button to end the conversation.

Washington DC

Dr. Gates is trying to reconnect his call with Dr. Johnson. He tries several times, but he can only get his voice mail. His hands are trembling, and he drops the phone. He says to himself, "What have I done? What have I done?"

Dr. Gates pulls himself together and travels to the White House, where the president meets with him.

"Hello, Mike."

"Hello, Mr. President."

"So why the urgency?"

"I got a call from Mark Johnson in China. He said that the Chinese took one of the viruses that we developed. And then it sounded like they arrested him. His phone went dead, and I haven't been able to get through to him since then."

"Wow. I'll get on top of this immediately and find out what's going on."

"Thank you, Mr. President. Also, the virus that Mark said they took is one that could make COVID-19 look like a minor annoyance."

"Thank you for bringing this to my attention."

That evening, Dr. Gates is in his home, trying to figure out what is going on, when the doorbell rings. He opens the door and finds a team of agents.

"Hello, what can I do for you?"

"Dr. Gates?"

"Yes."

"We are with Homeland Security, and you will have to accompany us."

"What's happening?"

"You are being investigated for subversive activities."

The agents escort Dr. Gates into their waiting SUV.

3

Washington DC

JENNIFER BARNES ANSWERS her cell phone. "Hello Jim, how're you doing?"

"Jenn, can we meet right now at the usual place?"

"Why all the cloak and dagger?"

"Have you ever seen the movie *The Manchurian Candidate*?"

"No."

The call ends abruptly. Jennifer tries to call him back, but the call will not go through. She hurries out the door to meet Jim at the coffee shop. As she approaches the shop, she sees Jim about to cross the street. She waves, and he waves back as he begins to cross the street. Suddenly, a vehicle speeds through the red light and runs Jim down before racing off.

Jennifer screams, "Oh, my God!" and runs over to James. He is obviously dead, and Jennifer cries uncontrollably.

Emergency vehicles begin to arrive, and some police officers interview Jennifer. Then a couple of men approach Jennifer, identify themselves as Homeland Security agents, and say they need to take her in for some additional questioning. The agents usher her toward their black SUV, and Jennifer has a flashback and does a double take; it's the same type of vehicle that killed James. She looks at the men, and when one of them turns such that she sees him in profile, she is shocked when she realizes that he looks just like the driver of the vehicle that hit James. She has a sense of foreboding and hesitates for a moment, then, falling back on her FBI training, she rapidly evaluates her options and says, "I really need to use the restroom first." She calmly walks over to the coffee shop and heads to the restroom; once inside, she opens the window she recalled being in the restroom and then squeezes through it.

After a few more minutes, the agents become suspicious, and one of them goes in to check on her. He returns, shaking his head, and says, "She's a real tricky one." The other agent speaks into the communications device attached to his jacket, saying, "She gave us the slip. Put out an APB on her."

As she walks quickly away, Jennifer tosses her cell phone into the bed of a pickup truck stopped at a traffic light.

She remembers where there is a store that sells DVDs and heads toward it. About twenty minutes later, she arrives at the store and goes inside. She walks over to where an employee is putting some DVDs on a shelf.

"Hi," she says.

"Hello," the clerk responds. "May I help you?"

"Yes, I'm looking for a movie."

"Which one?"

"*The Manchurian Candidate.*"

"That was put on the banned list a couple of months ago."

The employee pulls out a cell phone and quickly takes a picture of Jennifer. Jennifer is shocked and she exclaims, "Why did you do that?"

"I have to record any people asking for subversive material. What's your name?"

Jennifer turns and quickly heads out of the store.

A woman is walking some dogs. Jennifer quietly walks up behind her.

"Hi, Susan," she says.

The woman turns and recognizes her. "Jennifer, what are you doing here?"

"I'm in trouble."

"What do you want from me? I'm just a dog walker; you're the FBI agent."

"I need to see Bobby."

"Are you kidding me? He's doing everything he can to avoid the FBI and all of those black ops groups."

"That's why I need to see him; those black ops groups are after me."

"No way, not Ms. Perfect."

"Yes, and I'm really sorry for cutting off contact with you."

"I'll expect some additional groveling later, but I don't have direct contact with Bobby anymore. He said that he was getting too hot and that, for my own good, I should avoid contact with him."

"Isn't there any way to contact him?"

"He did give me one option, but only for a life-or-death emergency."

"Well, that's what I have. They killed Jim."

"Oh, my God, no!"

"Yes, and now they're after me. But I really want to find out why they killed Jim and make them pay for it."

"Okay, let's go to my apartment and figure it out."

Once inside Susan's apartment, they have some coffee, and Jennifer fills Susan in on what happened, and then she ends with, "So you can see why I want to get into contact with Bobby. I really need his expertise to help me figure out what is going on, while staying outside the reach of those black ops."

"Okay, let me explain how to get in contact with him. He insisted that nothing be written down, so turn on that memory of yours."

"Go ahead."

Jennifer listens attentively as Susan provides the details and then says, "Thank you so much. When this is all over, I will come back and do plenty of groveling, but I really need to get in contact with Bobby as soon as possible."

They hug, and then Jennifer leaves Susan's apartment and starts walking; after about half an hour, she arrives at an extremely retro-looking bookstore. She peers through the window, and seeing only one person in the store, she enters. She walks over to the woman in the store and says, "Hi, are you Maggie?"

"Yes, I am. How did you know?"

"I'm a friend of Bobby."

"Oh, and how can I help you?

"I'm looking for a copy of *1984*."

"That's been banned."

"I'm sorry, but I'm having trouble keeping up with all the books that have been banned. How about *Welcome to the Monkey House* by Kurt Vonnegut?"

"That's also been banned."

"I apologize. I think I'll just get a cup of coffee instead. Can you direct me to any place nearby?"

"I could use some coffee also. How about if I show you where it is?"

"That would be great, thanks."

They walk for almost an hour, with Maggie continually checking to make sure they aren't being followed, until they arrive at what looks like an abandoned warehouse. Maggie rings a bell, waits a moment, and then says, "Hi, we're fans of Eric and Kurt."

They hear a click, and Maggie opens the door. They walk through a maze of hallways until they arrive at a nondescript door. Maggie knocks four times, then three times, then two times, and then one final time. The door opens.

Maggie tells Jennifer, "It's okay, go ahead in. I have to head out now."

Jennifer tentatively walks through the door, which swings closed behind her. Then a wall panel slides open, and she hears a voice say, "Come in, Jennifer. It's been a long time."

She walks in to find a massive room filled with highly advanced computers and large video monitors, as well as her old friend Bobby. She is overwhelmed; it is almost like an arcade with video monitors in action all around her.

"Welcome to the dark side."

The song "On the Dark Side" begins to play. Jennifer smiles. Bobby walks up to her. She gives him a hug. Bobby smiles too.

"To what do I owe the pleasure?"

"I'm in trouble, and I need your help."

"Tell me more, pray tell."

Jennifer explains in detail everything that has happened and then says, "So I really need your help to figure all this out, while remaining out of the reach of the authorities."

"Well, you've come to the right place."

"But where did all of this equipment come from? It must have cost a fortune."

"Ah, Bitcoin and GameStop."

Jennifer smiles. "I see."

"Well, how about if we start with *The Manchurian Candidate*? I haven't seen it either."

"But it's been banned."

"Not on the dark side. Give me a moment, and I'll pull it up."

Bobby types on a keyboard and says, "We have a choice between the original and a remake. I don't like copies; let's do the original. How about some popcorn?"

"Sure."

Bobby prepares two large bowls of popcorn in a kitchen area. Then, they sit in a couple of comfortable chairs, and Bobby starts the movie on an extremely large monitor. The movie is very intense, and Jennifer feels emotionally drained.

At the end of the movie, Bobby says, "Well, I think we have your first answer."

4

Yulin Naval Base in Hainan, China

T HE UNDERGROUND TOP-SECRET naval base is
a hub of activity. Workers are rushing about working
on about a dozen submarines, with the focal point being a Type
093T submarine, an upgraded version of the Type 093 Shang-
class nuclear attack sub. The 093 is a second-generation attack
sub equipped with weaponry ranging from torpedoes to anti-ship
cruise missiles. A significant advancement with the 093 was in the
area of noise reduction, bringing it down to 110 decibels, which is
about in line with the improved US Los Angeles-class submarines.
The 093T was modified to handle special forces missions in coastal
waters, with those modifications including a wet docking hangar
for a swimmer delivery vehicle (SDV) and enhanced sonar, such as
a towed array sonar (TAS), as well as a propeller system designed
to be more effective in coastal waters where fishing nets and water
plants can cause problems.

In a private office on the base, several members of the Ministry
of State Security are gathered, including one agent dressed in a
biohazard suit. The most senior member says to the one in the

biohazard suit, "They will take you near the shore in the mini vehicle. Once you get established, visit as many highly populated areas as possible. Do not contact us until our unification goal has been accomplished. Until then, use your ATM card to cover your expenses. Remember your pledge to sacrifice everything for the Party and to never betray the Party."

The submarines are ready to sail, so the state security agent dressed in the biohazard suit boards the 093T. One by one, the subs begin to exit the underground base, with the 093T positioned to depart in the middle of the group.

Observing the Yulin Naval Base are a Japanese Taigai-class submarine, a US Los Angeles-class sub, and a US Virginia-class sub. The Taigai is the most advanced sub in the Japanese fleet, utilizing lithium-ion batteries to generate high speeds and to provide a highly advanced silent drive system, while its advanced sonar system enables it to track stealthier adversaries. The nuclear-powered Los Angeles has been a mainstay of the US submarine fleet for about half a century, going through a continuous rollout of upgrades, while the leading-edge nuclear-powered Virginia, with its full range of the most advanced systems, including such innovations as a high energy laser and photonic sensors (in place of a periscope), has been gradually replacing the Los Angeles. The Virginia was also designed to operate more effectively in coastal waters.

The Taigai sub follows the first Chinese sub departing the base, and the Los Angeles sub picks up the second Chinese sub.

The crew of the Virginia sub, utilizing the sub's Command, Control, Communications, Computers, Intelligence, Surveillance and Reconnaissance (C4ISR) capability, is monitoring all of the activity from a 360 degree perspective. The commanding officer says, "Let's stay here and see how many are in this parade."

After ten subs have departed from the naval bases, the navigator of the Virginia sub says, "The sixth sub has changed course from where it was heading initially; so far, it's the only one to change direction."

The CO responds, "And where is it heading?"

"Taiwan."

"That's interesting. Let's follow it."

"It has a TAS."

"Okay, let's plot an indirect course for the same destination. Exec, boost our speed as necessary."

About a day and a half later, the 093T and Virginia submarines have both arrived in the coastal waters of southern Taiwan, with the US sub still keeping its distance in order to try to avoid being detected. The Chinese sub appears to be carefully steering clear of the Zuoying Naval Yard, Taiwan's largest naval base, and any associated naval activity, while heading toward the port of Kaohsiung, a large civilian harbor south of the naval base.

On the US sub, the executive office says to the CO, "I'm assuming it's a 093T to be able to operate at this shallow depth."

"It should also have an SDV then. Could they be planning an onshore mission?"

"That would be bold, but to what purpose?"

"Well, let's see what happens next."

"It's amazing that Taiwan has virtually no submarine capability."

"But they do have the two World War II-era subs, which they bought from us about fifty years ago. And you can't overlook the other two subs they bought from the Netherlands forty years ago."

They both laugh.

Shortly thereafter, the Chinese sub surfaces, and the crew rapidly prepare the swimmer delivery vehicle for launch. A pilot for the SDV and the state security agent, both dressed in diving gear, exit the 093T, carefully move over to the SDV, and board it. It is then launched.

The surfacing of the Chinese sub and the launching of its SDV are being observed on the US sub via its photonic sensors.

The exec comments, "It's launched."

He is then interrupted by the navigator, who says, "Multiple hostiles approaching."

The CO commands, "Battle stations. Full speed and begin evasive maneuvers. Communicate the activity observed and request instructions."

Alarms are sounding; both internal and external communications are occurring, and the crew is scrambling to prepare for battle. The sub accelerates rapidly, trying to escape before it is trapped by the enemy.

About thirty minutes later, orders are sent to the sub, and the CO reads them out loud: "Do not engage. Repeat, do not engage. Return to normal activity."

The exec responds, "But what about the enemy? Is someone going to let them in on this?"

The navigator interjects with puzzlement, "Hostiles are breaking off."

The CO observes, "It looks like someone did let them in on this. But why?"

The exec comments, "I've never seen anything like this."

The CO orders, "Head back to our original observation position near the Yulin Naval Base."

Meanwhile, the SDV has reached a point near the shore of Kaohsiung, Taiwan's second largest city. The agent exits the SDV and swims toward shore, while the SDV heads back to the 093T. Once ashore, the agent discards his diving gear and begins walking toward the population center. As he walks, he thinks about how fortunate he is to have been chosen for such an important mission and how excited he is to be able to help the Party accomplish such an important goal.

When he reaches a populated area, he stops at the first ATM he finds in order to withdraw cash. Then he walks around looking for a mass transit station. When he finds one, he examines the route map, purchases a ticket, and boards one of the trains.

While riding on the train, he looks at the other people aboard the train and wonders why they would not gratefully accept and rejoice to become part of the People's Republic of China, soon to be the dominant world power and led by the all-powerful and all-knowing Communist Party. He concludes that their renegade leaders must have brainwashed them and forced them to oppose the PRC; re-education camps will teach them about the mistakes of their ways and the heinousness of their leaders, whom they will then recognize as enemies of the Party and impose upon them the most extreme penalties.

He reaches his stop and shifts his attention back to the mission at hand, looking forward to doing his all for the Party.

5

Washington DC

JENNIFER OBSERVES AS Bobby is searching on the internet. She comments, "I work for the FBI, and I've never been exposed to some of those sites you just accessed."

"As I told you before, you are on the dark side now. There is a lot of chatter about the feds pulling out all the stops to try to find someone; you, apparently."

"I still can't believe it. I went from trusted agent one moment to most wanted criminal the next."

"Well, you know my thoughts about what happens when we start giving up our freedoms."

"But what makes you think this is related to reduced freedoms?"

"It's all connected. We give up freedoms; the state takes more control. The state needs to control how we think and communicate in order to ensure the maintenance of its greater control; individuality is a threat and must be eliminated as much as possible. Eventually, the individual ceases to matter, except in the service of the state, and the state therefore can eliminate any individuals who rebel or pose any kind of threat to the state."

"You make it all seem so straightforward."

"It is. You're just not ready to accept it yet."

"But I am moving in your direction. I truly apologize for how I just dropped you in college. You are a true and loyal friend, and I was absolutely wrong to treat you like I did. I just got wrapped up in the idea of getting ahead and selfishly felt that being connected with you would hurt me. I'll never do anything like that again."

"Apology accepted," Bobby says, smiling. "Now let's see if we can get a better handle on what's going on. I will try the Renegades."

"Who are the Renegades?"

"A group of people like me. We coordinate to help each other."

Bobby types on his keyboard: "Renegades, consult requested."

"Aren't you concerned about security? Like what about the NSA?"

"We use dynamic encryption, with our own bells and whistles. It makes the alphabet soup, AES and RSA, as well as the fishes, seem like child's play."

Responses begin to come in on the large monitors surrounding them.

"Aussie here, mate."

"Rebel with a Cause, as well."

"Hi, Supergirl checking in."

"The Prisoner is on board."

Several others connect, and then Bobby says, "I have a friend in trouble at the highest levels. Have any of you picked up anything?"

There is a pause, and then Aussie responds, "I picked up one unusual item, but I don't think it would be connected to your friend; it was over in China. There was some top-security chatter about how they grabbed a Yank doctor named Johnson, Mark Johnson."

"Great, thanks Aussie."

"My Mandarin teacher should get some thanks as well."

Bobby wraps up by saying, "Everyone, please let me know if you pick up anything else."

The Renegades disconnect.

"Well, that's a start. I will dig into it and see where it leads."

After a few minutes of work, Bobby says, "Johnson is reportedly a top expert on viruses; he works for Dr. Michael Gates, the director of the National Institute of Allergy and Infectious Diseases here in DC. That's quite a mouthful. Ring any bells?"

"Well, I have heard of Gates, but not Johnson. I don't really know much about Gates, and Jim never mentioned either one."

"Okay, I'll keep digging."

Bobby does some more research and then says, "Gates reports to Dr. Samuel Page, the director of the National Institutes of

Health; Page just covered for him at a conference, indicating that Gates was indisposed."

"Like Gates, I have heard of Page, but I don't know anything about him."

"The presentation that Page covered for was titled 'The Next Viral Pandemic: What We Learned from COVID-19, and Should Gain of Function Research Be Considered?' This is getting very interesting."

"What is gain of function research?"

"This is where my work on conspiracy theories pays off. Gain of function research involves creating new, more dangerous viruses in order to study them. It's kind of like Frankenstein-type research, which leads to the obvious concern: what happens if it gets loose, like the monster did?"

6

Taiwan

THE CHINESE MINISTRY of State Security agent has reached the Zuoying train station for the high-speed railway. He buys a railway smart card and boards a train. The next stop is Tainan. He gets off the train there, quickly passes through several areas congested with people, and then boards the next train. He repeats this process at each additional stop: Chiayi, Yunlin, Changhua, Taichung, Miaoli, Hsinchu, Taoyuan, Banqiao, Taipei, and Nangang. He then gets a hotel room in Nangang before heading out to eat. As he sits in a restaurant, he thinks about how many lives he has likely saved; he figures thousands of Chinese soldiers have probably been saved, based upon the plan laid out in the Joint Island Attack Campaign. He smiles broadly from a feeling of great contentment.

South China Sea

After disengaging off the coast of Taiwan, the Virginia-class submarine is heading south to resume monitoring the Yulin Naval Base.

As it passes near Hong Kong, the navigator says, "We are being hailed by a British sub. It's an Astute and you won't believe this, but they are requesting that we receive a top-secret passenger."

The CO responds, "So how are they proposing to do this?"

"They request that lock-in/lock-out chambers be used on both sides so that everything can take place under water."

"It obviously must be important to them. Okay, tell them we agree. It's worth the price of admission to see this."

The nuclear-powered Astute-class submarine is the largest and most advanced of the Royal Navy's submarine fleet, with leading-edge systems in multiple areas, especially in regard to its Sonar 2076 system, which is possibly the best sonar system in the world.

The two submarines maneuver carefully, using their highly advanced systems and extremely experienced crews to position close to each other while avoiding a collision. When the subs are properly positioned, a single diver exits the UK sub and swims to the US sub, entering its lock-in/lock-out chamber. After entering the main body of the sub and removing his diving gear, the newly acquired passenger is taken to the commanding officer's quarters.

"Hello, I'm Commander Dawson."

"It's a pleasure to meet you, Commander. Smith is the name. I do apologize for the urgency and secrecy."

"Well, it did provide some entertainment for us. But I am obviously curious as to why it was necessary."

"I have some rather sensitive information, which is best delivered in person. First of all, though, I believe some credentials, in the form of a letter of introduction, are called for."

Smith pulls out a sealed envelope and hands it to Dawson, who opens the envelope and reads the letter inside, soon appearing to be impressed.

"You obviously have friends in high places."

"Yes, it goes with my line of work."

"MI-6?"

"Actually, a small, somewhat more secretive, group within MI-6."

"So with the introductions out of the way, can you tell me what is going on?"

"I am here to try to enlist your support."

"To what purpose?"

"We are planning a rather bold mission to rescue one of your countrymen from China, which is part of a bigger plan to avoid a very destabilizing takeover of Taiwan by China."

"And why have I not received orders regarding this from my government?"

"Well, that's a bit sensitive."

"In what way?"

"To be blunt, we believe that your leader is a dodgy and untrustworthy fellow."

Surprised, Dawson asks, "Can you be clearer?"

"We have rather unimpeachable evidence that your president is working with the Chinese Communist Party."

"What? Are you crazy?"

"Here, take a look at this."

Smith hands another, but larger, envelope to Dawson. He opens it and spends several minutes reviewing the contents and then says, "Let's say you have my attention."

"In addition, we observed your interaction with the local bullies near Taiwan, which was, would you not say, brought to a close in a somewhat unconventional manner."

"I would agree. And what is your explanation?"

"It obviously required very rapid coordination at the most senior levels, as well as a clear desire on the part of both sides not to disrupt the mission."

"Who are you planning to rescue?"

"Dr. Mark Johnson. One of our very well-placed assets let us know that Johnson was doing virus research with the Chinese, but that the Chinese decided to weaponize it and use it against Taiwan. They arrested Johnson when he discovered what they were doing."

"The sub that we trailed to Taiwan?"

"We believe so, which doesn't give us much time."

"I need more confirmation."

Dawson picks up his phone and says, "Send a message requesting information about Dr. Mark Johnson."

He then turns back to Smith and asks, "So what do you think is prompting the Chinese to act at this time?"

"Based on our intelligence, we believe they are trying to act preemptively before Taiwan begins to roll out its new modern submarine. As you know, Taiwan does not currently have an effective submarine fleet."

"Yes, my exec and I were talking about that earlier."

"As you probably know as well, China has used any and all means possible to stop Taiwan from acquiring modern submarines, and they were totally successful, to the point where Taiwan had to build its own. The first prototype is due to be rolled out in a few months, followed by a relatively rapid rollout of seven more subs. These will be leading-edge attack subs, each equipped with four dozen torpedoes, as well as anti-ship missiles. They will also be equipped with lithium-ion batteries for propulsion, making them virtually undetectable in the noisy waters of the Taiwan Strait."

"Yes, I was aware of most of that; it will obviously be a very big boost to Taiwan's defense."

"Exactly, and that boost to Taiwan's defense is the driving force behind China's current activity. It is relatively straightforward for many analysts to assume that China would continue to be in a position to dominate and easily defeat Taiwan, as China would still have about ten times as many submarines plus the rest of its massive military force."

"But you feel differently, and as a submarine commander, I understand where you are going with this, especially given our experience in these waters."

"Yes, we ran simulations with Taiwan having its full complement of eight new submarines and taking account of the noisy water conditions of the strait. We found that the likelihood of success for a Chinese invasion of Taiwan dropped from almost 100 percent to less than 50 percent."

"I get it. I can imagine how just eight modern submarines, used very effectively, could really disrupt an invasion. It's easy for those who haven't operated here to underestimate the challenge presented by these waters for a naval invasion."

"And what's probably even more important to the current situation is that China has run the same type of simulation and reached the same conclusion."

"So China needs to invade before the new subs are deployed."

"Precisely."

Soon thereafter, a reply message is delivered to Commander Dawson in his quarters, and he reads the response out loud: "'Confidential. Cease and desist.' Wow, an immediate escalation to a quasi-legal threat. They are obviously worried and trying to cover it up. It seems like it's time for defending against all enemies, foreign and domestic, to take precedence over obeying orders. So what's your plan?"

"To have some of our deep undercover agents lead one of our SBS teams from E Squadron into China; break out the doc; and make their way back to our sub. We then need to meet up with one of our ships; transfer the doc to the ship; and get him on a plane en route to England. Once in England, he can safely announce to the world what China has done with the virus."

"You Brits don't seem to mind living dangerously."

"It's worth the risk to stop China from taking Taiwan. With Taiwan, they would obviously control the South China Sea and totally dominate the region militarily."

"I understand the strategic significance, but I like missions to have a reasonable chance of success."

"Have you ever seen our SBS lads in operation?"

"No, I haven't."

"You should stop by Poole sometime and see how they train. I think you'd find they could teach your SEALS a thing or two. We are officially giving them a 50-50 chance, but I think they have a much better chance than that."

"And what are you looking for us to do?"

"We could really use your help for surveillance. Having you positioned strategically and utilizing your C4ISR could make the difference for us. We have to evade the enemy long enough to get the doctor airborne. We'll do all of the dirty work, but if you could be an additional pair of sharp eyes for us, the first round would definitely be on us."

"Okay, you've got a deal."

7

Washington DC

JENNIFER THINKS WHILE Bobby works on his computer, and then she says, "I need to do something useful; I can't just sit around."

"What are you thinking about doing?"

"Talking to Page to see if he has any idea what's going."

"But they're turning over every stone right now to find you."

"My training should help me avoid getting caught."

"How about if we boost your chances?"

"Your turn; what are you thinking?"

"Let's disguise you."

"With what?"

"I'll just order from a local store and have it delivered. I do it all the time. Here, let me pull up their website. What do you think about a gothic look?"

"No, thank you."

"Punk?"

"Nope."

"So I assume gothic-punk is out as well?"

"Now I remember why I cut you off."

Bobby looks a bit surprised. Jennifer says, "I'm sorry; I apologize. I'm a bit thrown off by this whole situation."

"No problem. I totally understand. And, actually, I like seeing the old Jennifer coming back. Here, you take over and make your selections."

"Okay, thanks."

When Jennifer is finished making her selections, Bobby places the order and then says, "We have an hour or two to kill. I'll put on a video."

Bobby starts a video, and Jennifer is amused to see a montage of videos and pictures from when they were in college.

"You're full of surprises."

"I thought you might enjoy it."

"You're right; I love it."

Jennifer watches a bit more, laughs, and says, "I almost forgot how much fun we use to have."

Then she sees James in a clip, and she begins to cry.

Bobby looks embarrassed. "I'm sorry; I should have used better judgment."

"It's okay. I feel sad seeing Jim because of what just happened to him, but I also feel good about seeing him during a happy time; it brings back such wonderful memories."

The costume is delivered, and Jennifer puts together her disguise, including a wig.

"Okay, I'm ready."

"Are you sure about this?"

"Yes. Seeing Jim in the video has motivated me even more to get to the bottom of this."

"You have Page's address?"

"Yes."

"Be careful."

"I will. Don't worry. Thank you for all of your help and for being such a great and forgiving friend."

"Returning safely will be thanks enough."

They hug, and Jennifer leaves. She begins walking down the street, warily monitoring whether anyone is following her. She makes a few changes of direction, and then, feeling confident no one is following her, she heads in the direction of Dr. Page's apartment.

After walking for almost an hour, Jennifer arrives at Dr. Page's apartment. It is late evening and she walks around the block a couple of times, checking whether anyone is watching the apartment. Not seeing anyone, she then watches for someone entering or leaving the building.

When she sees a man approaching the building, she walks quickly to catch up with him while she pretends to be talking on her phone, a clean one which Bobby gave to her, and searching in her purse, saying into the phone, "I'm looking, but I haven't found it yet."

The man uses a pass key to open the door to the building, and Jennifer, acting a bit exasperated with her imaginary search, grabs the door, smiles and says, "Thanks." The man nods, and they both head toward the elevator.

As they enter the elevator, Jennifer says into the phone, "I just can't find it. I'll call you later."

The man asks, "What floor?"

She smiles again and says, "Five, please."

"Are you new to the building?"

"Yes, I just moved in last week."

"I think you'll like it."

"I love it so far. Oh, here's my floor."

Jennifer exits the elevator and finds Dr. Page's apartment. She knocks on his door. He opens the door while looking somewhat puzzled and says, "Hello, can I help you?"

"Dr. Page?"

"Yes, and you are?"

Jennifer flashes her FBI badge and says, "I'm FBI Agent Barnes."

"What can I do for you?

"I'm here about Drs. Gates and Johnson. May I come in?"

"Yes, please. Have a seat. Would you like something to drink?"

"Thank you," Jennifer replies, "and nothing to drink, but thanks for offering."

"So why the interest in my colleagues?" Dr. Page asks.

"We have reason to believe that Dr. Johnson was doing research in China and has been arrested there. And he reports to Dr. Gates, who you just covered for at a conference because he was indisposed; can you elaborate on this?"

"Well," he explains, "I received an email from Dr. Gates saying he was ill and asking if I could do his presentation, which he forwarded to me. I didn't even know that Dr. Johnson was in China."

"Do you have any idea what Dr. Johnson might have been working on in China?"

"No, like I said, I didn't even know he was there."

"Can you tell me more about gain of function research, which was the topic of the presentation you gave in place of Dr. Gates? From my limited understanding, it seems potentially dangerous."

"It's extremely dangerous because it involves creating the most dangerous pathogens for laboratory study; there is the significant risk that something could go wrong, and a lethal pathogen could be unleashed on the public. I added a personal comment at the end of Dr. Gates presentation saying that I am absolutely opposed to such research."

"Was Dr. Gates in favor of gain of function research?" Jennifer asks.

"Yes. In fact, we recently had an argument about it, and I told him in no uncertain terms that I would not approve such research."

"Would he try to go around you?"

"No, we have worked—" Dr. Page stops, pauses, and then continues, "He wouldn't."

"Wouldn't what?" she pressed.

"They wouldn't do the research in China to get around my opposition. Johnson is also in favor of gain of function research, and he is Gates's top infectious disease researcher."

"Can you check with Dr. Gates as to whether they went around you and conducted the research in China?"

"Why wouldn't the FBI just ask him?"

"Generally, a friend or associate requesting information is more effective for gaining useful information; the target tends to let his, her or their guard down and becomes more forthcoming. In addition, being helpful with our investigation should definitely be a boost to your social credit score, and you know how much of a focus the current administration has on that."

"Okay, I'll give it a try. How can I get in contact with you?"

"I'll check back with you here, tomorrow evening, around this time."

"Why don't we just meet in your office?"

"I'm currently working undercover, and we're also trying to avoid any leaks, so we're keeping the circle very tight."

"Okay."

"Thank you for your help, Dr. Page."

"You're welcome."

Jennifer leaves; as she exits the building, she looks around for anyone who might be observing. She begins heading back to Bobby's place, once again using several directional changes to check if anyone is following her. After she arrives back at Bobby's place, she and Bobby hug.

"I was concerned that they might pick you up," he said.

"Everything went fine," she replied.

"What did you find out?"

"Gates and Johnson both were in favor of conducting gain of function research, but Page is opposed to it and prevented them from conducting the research here."

"Here?"

"They may have circumvented his opposition by conducting the research in China."

"So why did the Chinese arrest Johnson? Was he conducting the research without their approval?"

"No, research at that level couldn't be conducted without the explicit approval and significant involvement of the Chinese government."

"So why would they arrest him?"

"That's a very good question."

"Maybe they wanted to use the research for germ warfare, and Johnson found out and objected."

"You're way too wrapped up in conspiracy theories."

"Huh? Why are you here with me?"

"Good point."

"You said that Jim was part of the security detail for the president on his trip to China just before he was killed. During that trip, he could have found out the president was involved with the Chinese on this."

"This is beginning to feel like an espionage novel. Where is James Bond when we need him?"

"I'm surprised at you. His books and movies have just been banned. With thoughts like that, your social credit score is definitely heading south."

They both laugh.

8

Taiwan

A YOUNG BOY NAMED Jui-En is playing in Fushan Village, which is in the Zuoying District of Kaohsiung. He bounces a ball against a wall and tries to catch it when it bounces back toward him. Then Jui-En's younger sister and some other children join in, all trying to catch the ball and then throw it against the wall.

Later, Jui-En and his younger sister gather with their mother and father for dinner. The mother first serves her version of *Danzai* noodles, chewy wheat noodles in a seafood broth, with each serving being topped by a single shrimp. Everybody enjoys the noodle dish, and they talk actively about what they did during the day. Next, the mother serves *Tian bu la*, a fish tempura, which she prepared with a mild white fish, eggs, and tapioca flour; she prefers to use tapioca flour because it adds a little sweetness, which the children like. Everybody enjoys the second course as well, and the children begin to talk about how they are looking forward to dessert. As they finish the last of the Tian bu la, the mother gets up to serve dessert. The children close their eyes, which is their little family tradition, and the mother serves a dessert of *Douhua*, a traditional tofu pudding, which she prepares with brown sugar syrup for added sweetness. The children open their eyes and excitedly look at the Douhua. They begin to eat it, while making funny faces at each other and laughing.

After dinner, the children prepare for bed. Their mother tucks them in while they talk about the fun they are going to have tomorrow.

In the morning, Jui-En awakens with a cough and a fever. He tells his mother that his muscles hurt. She is concerned and tells him to stay in bed. She takes care of him during the day, but his symptoms continue to worsen, and she becomes increasingly concerned.

When her husband returns in the evening, she expresses her concern to him and asks him to take Jui-En to see a doctor. He takes his son to a local outpatient clinic. These clinics are typically crowded, but it is especially crowded tonight. The doctors and nurses seem overwhelmed and panicked by the sudden increase in the number of patients. With the obvious expectation of a long wait to see a doctor, Jui-En's father tries to make him as comfortable as possible, which poses a real challenge with the overflow in the normally uncomfortable waiting area.

After a few hours, they finally get to see a doctor, who examines Jui-En and shakes his head. He indicates that it seems like the flu, and it's in line with what he's been seeing with other patients today, but the quickness with which it has hit the area and the rapid increase in the severity of the symptoms has him perplexed. The doctor tells him to keep Jui-En in bed and to have him drink plenty of fluids.

Washington DC

It is morning, and Bobby is working on his computer, examining various live videos of the Washington DC area. Jennifer awakens and goes over to see what he is doing. She comments, "Videos of DC?"

"Yes, we need to coordinate for your mission tonight. We can't have you just run off like last night, with no idea what's going on out there."

"So what's your idea?"

"You're going to have a communications device so we can stay in contact, and I'm going to have a visual on you as much as possible."

"And you're going to use these videos?"

"Yes, these are feeds from the traffic cameras throughout DC. I'm coding a program to track your movement with my video automatically changing from one camera feed to another as you move through the city."

"Stalkers would love this."

"What a devious mind you have."

"Just a result of my training."

"Also, I have other monitors set up to automatically track the surrounding area, in case you run into any trouble."

"It's nice to have you on my side."

"Let's test the communications device."

Jennifer attaches the communications device to her ear, and they do a test. It works well in their test, and Bobby says, "It should easily cover the distance to Page's apartment and back, plus more distance if necessary; I have it coordinated to tap into repeaters as necessary. And I'm using my encryption technology to avoid any snooping."

"Like I said, it's nice to have you on my side."

They both smile.

Later, after some dinner, Jennifer heads out.

"I have you on video. How is the audio for you?"

"It's great; you're coming through crystal clear."

"I also tapped into the video security system of Page's apartment building, so I'll be able to monitor the public area."

"Good work."

About an hour later, Jennifer is approaching the apartment building and reports, "I'm arriving."

"I've tapped into the door security system as well. Let me know when you're ready, and I will unlock it for you."

"Great, thanks. Give me a moment to get to the door." She walks up to the door and then says, "Okay, I'm ready."

She hears a click and then she opens the door.

"That was convenient, thanks."

"You're welcome."

She heads to Dr. Page's apartment and knocks on the door. He opens the door and invites her in, but he seems nervous.

"Thank you," she says as he closes the door. "Are you okay?"

"Yes, thanks."

"Were you able to get in contact with Dr. Gates?"

"I tried but couldn't find him. I got some unusual reactions when I asked around about him. I'm not sure what's going on and what else I can do."

"Okay. Thanks for trying."

She begins walking to the door. Just then, Bobby breaks in and announces, "You have company. You need to leave immediately."

She rushes out of the apartment.

"They're coming up on the elevator. Take the stairs."

She runs to the stairwell and heads down as quickly as she can.

"Someone's at the front door; head out the back door. It's an emergency exit, so it will set off the alarm."

As she pushes through the back door, the alarm sounds.

An agent at the front door says into his communication device, "She must have used the emergency exit," and he runs around the building, while those who went up on the elevator head back down.

Jennifer jumps over a fence and runs down the street.

Bobby says, "Vehicles are converging from multiple directions. There is a Metro station a block ahead."

She runs at top speed and reaches the station just as a train is arriving. She uses her SmarTrip card to enter the system, runs to the train and jumps aboard, and then sits in a seat which has its view from the outside blocked. As she catches her breath, the train begins to depart. She then breathes a big sigh of relief and her heart rate begins returning to normal.

Several vehicles are speeding around the area that Jennifer just passed through, and multiple men are running around the area.

After a few stops, Jennifer exits the train. She makes her way back to Bobby's place in a roundabout way. When she reaches Bobby, she hugs him and then says, "Thank you so much. I wouldn't have gotten away without your help."

"You're very welcome. I'm just glad that you're safe."

9

Taiwan

T HE HEALTH CARE system is overwhelmed. People throughout heavily populated western Taiwan are flooding outpatient clinics, doctors' offices, and hospitals with severe and rapidly escalating flu-like symptoms. Doctors and nurses are struggling to deal with the sudden massive influx of patients. Hospital beds are filled with the most severe cases. Given the flu-like symptoms, doctors have been trying Tamiflu as a possible treatment, but due to the sudden spike in the number of patients, supplies of Tamiflu are already running low; furthermore, Tamiflu seems at best to be able slow the progression of the disease, but not reverse it.

A mobile infectious disease team, a joint effort between the Taiwan Centers for Disease Control and some teaching hospitals, arrives at a hospital in Taipei, and the team immediately goes into action. They deliver additional personal protective equipment for the hospital and begin evaluating and enhancing the disease control practices throughout the hospital, including, for example, measuring the negative pressure of isolation rooms; it is critical to maintain lower air pressure in the isolation rooms so that contaminated air does not flow outside.

The government is rapidly leaning into the lessons it learned from the SARS outbreak of 2002-2004, and which proved highly effective during the COVID-19 pandemic. During the SARS outbreak, Taiwan had the highest fatality rate (over 20 percent) of any country with more than ten cases. Taiwan was able to significantly improve its relative performance during the COVOD-19 pandemic, which is rather impressive given its proximity to the location of the initial outbreak.

The government declared a health emergency and activated the Central Epidemic Control Center. The CECC is an agency of the National Health Command Center and is associated with the Centers for Disease Control. It has broad authority to coordinate efforts across various government agencies and enlist additional resources if necessary. It immediately implemented the following strategies: a surveillance and reporting system in order to accurately track and monitor the spread of the new disease; isolation of those infected, with as many of them as possible placed in the specially designed hospital isolation rooms; rigorous contact tracing to identify any individuals who may have been exposed to the disease and the immediate quarantining of such individuals;

the mandatory wearing of face masks; and mass mobilization of temperature screening.

Jui-En's family is mourning his death. The remaining members of his family are already feverish and coughing.

The rapidly rising death toll is creating panic, as people are realizing the lethality of the disease. The public is demanding action and solutions. The government is pushing its disease experts to do everything possible to combat the new disease.

Scientists within the Division of Preparedness and Emerging Infectious Diseases, part of the Centers for Disease Control, have been working feverishly to analyze the new pathogen. They quickly identified it as an influenza virus and then immediately focused on the uniqueness of the virus, where they zeroed in on the polymerase basic protein 2 (PB2) and hemagglutinin (HA).

For PB2, which is involved in viral replication within the host cell, they found the well-known 627K substitution, which is essentially a mutation involving lysine being substituted at residue, or molecular unit, position 627 of the protein. This mutation, which occurred with the influenza virus responsible for the pandemic of 1918, and has also been included in many subsequent flu viruses, leads to a significant increase in the virulence of the virus in mammals. They also found other PB2 mutations known or expected to increase virulence, including T271A, Q591K,

D701N, and S714R. In addition, they discovered some previously unknown or uninvestigated mutations.

For HA, which is a key binding protein for influenza, they found the D222G mutation, which involves the substitution of glycine for aspartic acid and results in a significant increase in lethality. Once again, they also discovered some previously unknown or uninvestigated mutations.

As the scientists conducted in vitro and then in vivo studies of the virus, they became increasingly alarmed. The viral mutations seemed to operate synergistically, dramatically increasing both the contagiousness and the severity, especially the lethality, of the associated disease. It was as though the virus had been designed to be as dangerous as possible.

The findings of the scientists caused the CECC to request an immediate lockdown of the country. This was quickly approved and communicated by text message to all cell phones in Taiwan, as well as through other media. Transportation throughout Taiwan was dramatically curtailed. Even though Taiwan is excluded from the World Health Organization, an immediate notification was sent to the WHO in order to alert the rest of the world of the outbreak.

10

THE REST OF the world is becoming increasingly concerned. Travel to and from Taiwan has essentially ceased, and aggressive contact tracing is being conducted for anyone who has had any recent contact with anyone from Taiwan. Thus far, no cases of the new disease have occurred anywhere outside of Taiwan, but everyone is on edge, especially having just recently overcome COVID-19.

Debate about the outbreak in Taiwan is occurring in the United Nations and within the World Health Organization. With Taiwan unrepresented in both international organizations, it is unable to defend itself as China blames it for the outbreak and pushes aggressively to totally isolate it from the rest of the world. No one is defending Taiwan.

China continues to escalate its verbal aggression against Taiwan, claiming that it will use any and all means necessary to make sure that the disease doesn't spread beyond Taiwan. The government of Taiwan attempts to protest, but lacking a significant platform and any meaningful interest from most of the rest of the world, its protest is barely noticed and definitely unheeded. With the world still battle-weary, after having recently fought against COVID-19, there is a general willingness on the part of most countries, whose populations are intent on maintaining their relatively recent return to normal life, to step aside and give China the authority to lead the new disease battle, especially with China being so incredibly willing to take charge.

South China Sea

The US and UK submarines are approaching Hainan.

Aboard the US sub, British agent Smith tells Commander Dawson, "I will have to head back to our sub to lead the rescue mission."

"I certainly don't envy you that mission."

"It's all in a day's work."

"Well, we'll do what we can to help on the surveillance side. The communications could be a little tricky, but we'll make it work."

"I appreciate your help."

"Good luck."

"Thanks; save me a cold one, mate."

"Will do."

They smile and shake hands.

Smith puts on his diving gear and gets into the lock-in/lock-out chamber, ready to return to the UK sub. The chamber is opened to the ocean, and he swims back. Once aboard the UK sub, he updates the commander and then coordinates with his eight-member Special Boat Service (SBS) team.

Smith instructs the SBS team, "Okay, lads, the Yanks will be supporting us, but it's really up to us. We will meet up with our in-country agents onshore, and they will guide us in. We want to get in and out as quickly, and with as little mess, as possible. Stay alert, and watch your mates."

Smith and his SBS team, dressed in their diving gear, enter a hangar in order to access the swimmer delivery vehicle. The hangar is sealed, flooded, and then opened to the ocean. The SDV, with the capacity for a crew of six, is maneuvered onto its launch pad, and then Smith plus five members of the SBS team board the SDV, with one team member assuming the role of pilot and another the role of navigator. The remaining three members of the SBS team will stay with the sub and help handle the retrieval of the SDV when the mission is completed. With the six-member crew aboard, the SDV is released to begin its trip.

The UK sub was able to get relatively close to Hainan, but it will still be about a two-hour trip for the SDV, a leading-edge US-made Mark 11 Shallow Water Combat Submersible, which has advanced computer and navigation systems, including an electro-optical periscope and sonar detectors. The SDV is battery powered, providing critically needed stealth for commando missions such as this.

The pilot and navigator are very focused on operating the SDV, but the rest of the crew has a lot of thinking time, with which they focus on their plan, including contingency strategies, but particularly on how they will succeed; there is no room in their thinking for anything like the fear of failure. They are part of what is arguably the most highly trained commando group in the world, and that is reflected in their confidence and their mindset.

About an hour into their trip, a patrol ship is picked up by the SDV's radar detector, and the electro-optical periscope is used to observe it. The navigator and the pilot coordinate a maneuver to maintain sufficient distance from the ship in order to avoid possible detection.

Later, as they approach the shore, they use the electro-optical telescope again to check the shore area. Observing no significant activity, they proceed to their designated landing zone, where they all jump out and push the SDV to a location where it will remain during the land-based portion of their mission. With the mission taking place at night, darkness will greatly reduce the risk of the

SDV being discovered. They take off their diving gear and leave it with the SDV.

Smith pulls out a GPS device to locate the in-country agents who are to guide the team in. He finds that they are about a mile away, and he uses a hand signal to start his team moving toward them, while also communicating to the agents that they are heading in their direction. They soon reach the two agents, who are dressed in Chinese police uniforms and sitting in two black SUVs with tinted windows. The team piles into the SUVs, and they head off.

Smith, sitting in the front passenger seat of the lead SUV, asks the agent driving, "Can you update me?"

"They still have Johnson in their off-site location, a small house not far from here. They are avoiding their official facilities because they are trying to keep word from spreading that they have a Yank."

"It's nice of them to make our job so much easier. And great work on your part."

"Thanks. It really helps that the Benjamins still rule in China."

"How many of the enemy should we expect?"

"They have varied between about a dozen and a half dozen, with more during the day and fewer at night."

"As we planned, you and your partner will get them to open the door, and we'll take over from there."

"How well armed are they?"

"They have hardly anything; they just don't seem to be expecting any kind of rescue attempt."

The SUVs arrive at the house where Johnson is being held, and the team quietly moves to the front door. The two agents dressed in police uniforms knock on the front door, while Smith and his team conceal themselves on the side. One of the occupants of the house comes to the front door and looks through the peephole. Seeing what appear to be two police officers, he opens the door without any concern. Smith and his team rush in, and the last agent in closes the door. Smith and his team are highly skilled in hand-to-hand combat, and they quickly subdue the opposition without the need to fire a shot and without any casualties.

A very startled Dr. Johnson says, "Who are you?"

Smith responds, "We're the good guys, and it's time to get you out of here."

"British?"

"Yes, but we are getting some assistance from the Yanks."

The SBS team ties up their opponents. They all head out of the house and get back into the SUVs.

Smith directs Johnson into the lead vehicle, and Smith himself gets back into the front passenger seat. He tells the driver, "Take it easy. We don't want to get pulled over for anything."

"It will be just like a Sunday drive."

Smith then turns to Johnson and says, "We have a bit of an adventure ahead for you. We are going to start in a mini sub and then move aboard a full-size sub. The transfer will occur underwater, so we will be wearing diving suits. Have you ever dived?"

"I tried it once, but I can't say I was very good at it."

"Don't worry, we are, and we will guide you through it."

They soon arrive back where they left the SDV. As they are getting out of the SUVs, a police car drives by and catches them in its headlights. The car does a quick U-turn.

Smith says, "It looks like we have company." He then tells his agents in police uniforms, "You take the lead, and we'll jump in as necessary."

The police car pulls up and stops. There are two officers in the car; the one on the passenger side is talking into a communications device. They get out of their car, and the agents walk up to them and greet them. They talk for a few moments, and then the agents attack the police officers. They knock out the officers and place them back in their car.

One of the agents says to Smith, "They called in before we took care of them, so there will be more of them on the way."

"Okay, let's wrap up quickly and be on our way."

Smith turns to one of the members of the SBS team who is British Chinese and says, "Sorry we can't fit you in for the return trip. Hopefully, it won't get too tricky for you here. We'll extract you as soon as possible."

"Don't worry, I'll be fine, but you are definitely buying the first round."

"Absolutely, mate."

They shake hands.

Smith also shakes hands with the two agents and comments, "You guys were brilliant. Stay safe, and let us know what we can do for you."

One of them replies, "Will do, but let's get out of here." The other agent nods, and Smith nods as well.

The agents drive off in the SUVs, accompanied by the SBS team member remaining behind, and Smith and the rest of the team hurry toward the SDV, pulling Johnson along. Police cars begin arriving with their sirens blaring.

When Smith and the rest of the group reach the SDV, they put on their diving gear and help Johnson with his gear. Before they can push the SDV back into the water, the patrol boat they avoided on the way in shines a light in their direction, catching them in the light.

Smith says, "Another complication. Let's move."

They push the SDV into the water and get in, with Johnson being assisted again. The pilot and the navigator are intensely focused, as they work together to figure out how to get away from the patrol boat. As they head toward their mother boat, they veer off their preferred path whenever necessary to avoid detection by the patrol boat, which is using sonar to try to find them, while the SDV is using its sonar detectors to avoid the patrol boat. It is like a game of cat-and-mouse. The pilot and navigator know the patrol boat will likely eventually find them, but they are trying at least to delay that moment as long as possible.

The SDV continues maneuvering, but then the patrol boat's radar detects them.

The navigator says to the pilot, "They have us."

"What do you think?"

"I don't know, but if they have any, it's going to get rather hairy."

"We'll find out soon enough. In the meantime, let's pull out all the stops."

The SDV sharply changes direction. A barrel-like device plunges into the water, and moments later, it explodes, rocking the SDV violently. The noise is deafening.

The pilot says, "We won't last long like this."

"But they can't have too many on a patrol boat."

"Enough to take care of us."

Suddenly, there is a massive explosion. The SDV rocks even more violently this time and barely holds together. The patrol boat has been blown out of the water.

The navigator exclaims, "They got it."

The pilot adds, "The cavalry to the rescue."

"I'm plotting an intercept course."

"Yes, I've had enough of this for one day."

The SDV heads toward the UK sub. As the SDV approaches the sub, the hangar door is opened, and the three SBS team members who remained behind plus some divers from the sub work as quickly as possible to retrieve the SDV. A couple members of the SBS team help Johnson through the process, and soon they are all aboard the sub.

On the US sub, the navigator says, "Multiple enemy ships heading in our direction. It looks like they're throwing everything they have into this."

Commander Dawson replies, "Let our British friends know and plot a course out of here for them, as well as us."

Aboard the UK sub, the executive officer tells the commanding officer, "The Yanks have picked up a lot of unfriendly company approaching."

Commander Dawson asks his executive officer and navigator, "So how does it look?"

They both shake their heads no.

The exec replies, "Given the positioning of everyone and the need on the British side for their boat to meet up with their ship, we don't have a good solution. It looks like we could be heading toward a standoff."

Dawson says, "I hope you're ready for some excitement."

They all force themselves to smile a bit, while also doing a bit of shoulder shrugging and head tilting. They are mentally preparing for the challenge ahead of them and trying to buck up each other.

Dawson adds, "Let our British friends know the situation as we see it."

On the UK sub, the exec passes along to the CO, "The Yanks can't figure a way out."

"Okay, let's pull out all the stops and see if we can win the race. Let all of our friends know that we're going full out."

The exec communicates to the engineer officer, "Flank speed. Give us everything you have."

He responds, "Aye aye."

The exec then has the CO's message passed along.

The subs are moving as fast as possible to meet up with the UK ship, which has also accelerated its speed to help close the gap. The ship is a Queen Elizabeth-class aircraft carrier, which is often described as a supercarrier due to its size and considered to be essentially a floating military base.

Chinese ships are racing to intercept the UK aircraft carrier, as directed by Chinese Naval Intelligence, which intercepted communications indicating that the UK sub carrying Johnson is heading to meet up with the aircraft carrier. The closest Chinese ship is a Type 052D destroyer, also known as a Luyang III-class destroyer, which is a guided missile destroyer and considered to be a multi-role destroyer due to its capability for anti-ship, land attack, surface-to-air, as well as anti-submarine warfare.

The US sub reaches the UK aircraft carrier. Commander Dawson says, "Let them know that we will be joining them."

The exec interjects, "And it looks like a Luyang destroyer will be the first to crash our party."

"Yes, it's becoming so hard to keep the riffraff away."

The US sub executes a semicircular maneuver in order to accompany the aircraft carrier.

About twenty minutes later, they meet up with the UK sub, and both subs surface.

The CO of the UK sub says, "Let them know we're ready for the transfer."

Smith tells Johnson, "It's time for you to move on. We're going to do a helicopter transfer. It's a bit tricky, but our lads are well trained, so you'll be in good hands. If it wasn't so urgent, we'd keep you on the sub and not put you through this, but getting you out quickly could make all the difference." Johnson understandably looks a bit nervous. "When we get you to a safe location, we need you to publicly spill the beans on this whole affair."

"After what they put me through, no one will be able to hold me back."

"Brilliant, mate."

Aboard the aircraft carrier, an AW159 Wildcat helicopter is being prepped. The AW159 is an extremely versatile helicopter, capable of conducting a wide range of operations from various types of warfare to command and control, as well as troop transfer and search and rescue.

The carrier's commanding officer says, "Let's get this done quickly, before things get out of control here."

The AW159 takes off, heading toward the UK sub.

Aboard the US sub, the exec says, "Here comes the Luyang."

The CO thinks for a moment and then responds, "Let's try to head it off."

"You like to live dangerously."

"Why should the Brits have all the fun? Besides, we just need to buy them a little time."

The US sub heads off in the direction of the Chinese destroyer.

The helicopter reaches the UK sub and lowers a basket. Several members of the crew, as well as Smith and Johnson, are on the deck of the sub. The water is a bit choppy, but the crews of both the helicopter and the sub operate flawlessly, and Johnson is loaded into the basket, which then is raised up and Johnson is assisted into the helicopter. The helicopter begins flying back to the aircraft carrier.

Aboard the US sub, the exec exclaims, "They're prepping a missile."

The CO commands the weapons officer, "Intercept it."

The Chinese destroyer fires a missile at the helicopter, and the sub fires a high-energy laser at the missile, intercepting it just before the missile reaches the helicopter. The missile explodes, causing the helicopter to lurch about violently, but the experienced pilot is able to regain control.

On the deck of the UK sub, Smith shakes his fist in the air and exclaims, "Well done, Yanks."

The helicopter lands on the deck of the aircraft carrier, and Johnson is rapidly transferred to a T-45C Goshawk, an aircraft carrier-capable modified version of the British Aerospace Hawk jet trainer. A T-45C, which has been the staple jet aircraft trainer of the US Navy, was being tested by the Royal Navy, when some quick thinking and amazing logistics work got the plane to the aircraft carrier just in time for the current mission. UK pilots have trained on Hawk jets for decades, so flying the Goshawk is very much a layup for them.

The challenge was where to fly the Goshawk, given its limited range of eight hundred miles. Some quick diplomatic maneuvering and top-secret negotiations yielded a solution: Vietnam. Military cooperation between the UK and Vietnam has reached a significant level, having really been kicked into higher gear in late 2018 with the signing of a geospace cooperation agreement between the two countries, accompanied by discussions of additional cooperation across multiple dimensions, including their respective militaries. As part of this attitude of cooperation, Vietnam also very quickly signed a free trade agreement with the UK following Brexit. The increasing closeness of their relationship during the early 2020s, combined with increasing territorial disputes between Vietnam and China, made possible this top-secret agreement to allow the Goshawk to land in Vietnam in order to transfer their highly sensitive passenger to a longer distance-capable plane.

The pilot is seated in the front student seat, and Johnson is in the back instructor seat of the Goshawk. The pilot starts the takeoff, quickly ramping up to about 140 miles per hour, and then they are airborne. The crew of the carrier is cheering, enjoying the feeling of success.

The plane is gaining altitude when a Chinese Type 072III landing ship appears on the horizon, with a large weapon mounted on its bow. The weapon is an electromagnetic railgun, which uses electrical currents to generate magnetic fields, which, in turn, propel a sliding metal conductor to fire projectiles at speeds of greater than Mach 5. The railgun begins to fire at the Goshawk.

The plane is hit and explodes violently. The carrier crew shifts from elation to dejection.

Smith has been monitoring the situation from the sub and shouts, "You bloody bastards!"

Commander Dawson, also observing, remains stoic.

11

The South China Sea

COMMANDER DAWSON RECEIVES a message requesting an explanation for his actions. Clearly frustrated, he says, "Tell them I'm doing my job; I'm defending Americans and American interests."

A short while later Dawson receives another message. He says to the exec, "I've been relieved; you're in charge."

"I fully support you, so they're going to have to relieve me also."

"No, this is all on me. Especially now, we need as many good men as possible in leadership positions."

The exec understands and shakes his head in agreement.

Washington DC

It is morning, and Bobby is eating some cereal while he is working on his computer. Jennifer awakens. She walks over to Bobby and greets him, "Hard at work already."

"The early hacker gets the password."

"That looks good; I think I'll have some." Jennifer gets some cereal also and sits next to Bobby. "So what are you trying to do?"

"I'm just doing a little prepping to infiltrate the spooks."

"And how are you planning to do that?"

"Remember the SolarWinds hack?"

"Of course, but they've had years to clean up their systems."

"They cleaned what they could find, and the hackers left plenty of obvious things for them to deal with, but that was all to divert attention away from the real long-term strategy of putting in place deeply hidden backdoors, which they can use anytime they choose to access the most sensitive and secure systems."

"But wasn't that a Russian government-run operation? Why would they give access to you?"

"They wouldn't, but hackers are naturally a bit devious and often looking to make a buck, or millions of bucks."

"So how would you find them? How much would it cost?"

"Finding them is not too difficult; you've obviously heard about the dark web. But negotiating a deal with them is a bit more challenging; they want a lot of money, which I have, plus confidence that their backdoor won't be compromised or resold."

"But they're not just out there advertising on the dark web for anyone to see."

"You are correct." Bobby points at his screen. "To access the dark web, I use the Onion browser; it's still the best Tor-powered browser." The dark web pops up on Bobby's screen, and he copies a URL into the browser. "I got this from one of my contacts; that's what I was doing earlier."

A website pops up on his screen, offering computer security services. There are numerous options available and Bobby clicks on a tab specifying "Ultra-premium Level Personal Consultation," and the response is a request for the payment of ten thousand dollars in Bitcoin and an IP address. Bobby provides both, with an automated Bitcoin calculator determining the exact amount of Bitcoin required for a payment of ten thousand dollars.

Jennifer asks, "Now what?"

"Now we wait while they evaluate my IP address; they want to make sure I can be trusted, that I'm a real hacker, not a government agent, and that I can act professionally so as to not compromise their backdoor."

"Ten thousand dollars is really cheap for the ability to access government websites."

"The ten thousand dollars is just the charge to be evaluated as a potential purchaser of access to one of their backdoors. If I don't pass muster, they keep the ten thousand, and I don't hear back from them."

"That sounds like a scam."

"Welcome to the dark web."

About an hour later, Jennifer says, "It looks like you haven't met their requirements."

"You need to have patience. Pretend that you're a doctor."

"Ha ha, now I really remember why I cut you off."

They both smile, and then a response appears on the computer screen: "Deposit $500,000 in Bitcoin."

Bobby deposits the half-million dollars and receives the backdoor in a highly encrypted format.

Jennifer is puzzled. "But it's encrypted."

"Yes, but their evaluation indicated that I can handle that level of encryption. If I needed a lower level of encryption, the price would have been much higher, or they might have passed entirely."

Bobby engages his decryption algorithm and is presented with a website, a username, and a long list of numbers and letters forming a password. Bobby uses the information and gains access to the most secure portion of the US National Cybersecurity and Communications Integration Center's computer system. The center is a division of the Department of Homeland Security's Cybersecurity and Infrastructure Security Agency, and it has access to highly secret information across a range of systems, including those of the Department of Defense, the Federal Bureau of Investigation, and the National Security Agency.

Bobby exclaims, "Wow, this is the mother lode. We can access anything from here. What have you always wanted to know?"

"What do you mean?"

"Like who killed JFK or does Area 51 really have aliens?"

"Hmm, I'd really like to know what the last message on Kryptos is. I guess it's a part of the natural rivalry between the FBI and CIA that I still have; once a member, always a member. But we can do that later; first things first. We need to find out what's going on with Gates."

"All work and no play."

"Sorry, just delayed."

"Okay, I'll get on with it."

Bobby works for over an hour, searching through various areas of the center's system and accessing other connected systems. Jennifer gets in some stretching, which helps her to relax a bit.

Finally, he says, "I have it. It took a lot of digging; they're trying to keep it under wraps. But I finally found it in a subversives file."

"What does it say?"

"Here, take a look; I'm going through it now."

Jennifer comes over and observes.

Bobby continues, "It says that he was arrested for engaging in activities intended to undermine the US government. He is being held in isolation; no visitors and not even an attorney allowed."

"Where is he being held?"

"In a Homeland Security detention center here in DC. It's not a very high security center; apparently, they aren't very worried about him trying to escape or someone breaking him out."

"It makes sense, though, if they're trying to keep him under the radar."

"There isn't much in the way of additional details."

"It looks like I'll have to talk to him, then."

"Are you kidding?"

"No, but I will definitely need your help again."

"What are you thinking?"

"Well, first I need to do some reconnaissance. What is the address?"

United Nations

The Security Council is debating a Chinese proposal for China to take control of Taiwan in order to prevent the spread of the new disease beyond Taiwan. The Permanent Representatives to the United Nations, generally called UN ambassadors, of the fifteen member nations currently sitting on the Security Council, including the five permanent members (China, France, Russia, the United Kingdom, and the United States), are involved in a very lopsided and contentious debate.

The Chinese ambassador says, "The People's Republic of China is willing and able to bear this tremendous burden to prevent the world from having to go through another pandemic. You should be elated that we are willing to take on the risk necessary to protect your people. All that you have to do is sit back and receive the benefit, but instead you choose to return to your colonial roots of interference in the affairs of China, still seeking to exercise some control over the South China Sea. Was not a ninety-nine-year so-called lease forced upon China by your country enough for you?"

The UK ambassador responds, "The government of the United Kingdom believes that the People's Republic of China is seeking to take advantage of a humanitarian crisis in order to achieve a long-sought-after strategic goal, and that the outbreak in Taiwan can be effectively addressed without the need for a takeover by the PRC."

The US ambassador interjects, "If we allow another worldwide pandemic to occur so soon after COVID-19, there will be hell to pay."

The UK ambassador says, "I am beginning to understand how the Henry Fonda character in your American film *12 Angry Men* felt, but as we learned from that film, being outnumbered is not the same thing as being wrong."

The US ambassador says, "How about if we take a break to let everybody calm down a bit?"

A break is agreed to.

The US and Chinese ambassadors have a brief side discussion. The US ambassador says, "Let's use the Suez strategy; we'll just go to a vote here and then push the full UN, where the UK doesn't have a veto, to take up the issue." The Chinese ambassador nods in agreement.

The Security Council reconvenes, and the council moves to a vote.

After the vote is taken, the president of the Security Council states, "There were fourteen votes in favor and one vote opposed. The draft resolution has not been adopted, owing to the negative vote of a permanent member of the Security Council."

The meeting of the Security Council is adjourned, and the attendees begin to disperse, with the US and Chinese ambassadors engaged in a conversation as they exit the meeting.

The UK ambassador is observing this after having exercised the UK's veto. The ambassador then turns to a close aide and says, "It appears as though we're just delaying the inevitable, but at least we're buying our people some more time. Maybe they can pull a rabbit out of the hat."

12

Beginning in the South China Sea

FOLLOWING THE DESTRUCTION of the Goshawk plane, the various ships and boats dispersed, with neither side choosing to continue the encounter. The UK submarine and aircraft carrier are traveling together.

On the sub, Smith is communicating with his headquarters. "Line up the connections," he says. "I'll get started immediately."

The sub and the carrier stop, and a helicopter transfer is carried out once again, but this time with Smith as the passenger. Once he's aboard the carrier, he gets into an F-35B, which is the staple single-seat combat jet of the Queen Elizabeth-class aircraft carrier, due to the plane's short takeoff and vertical-landing capabilities. Smith takes off and heads west toward Vietnam, which is easily reachable with the F-35B's thousand-mile range. He is planning to take advantage of the secret agreement with Vietnam to allow transit through one of its air force bases. With its supersonic speed, the plane reaches the base in southern Vietnam in under an hour, whereupon Smith immediately switches to a Eurofighter Typhoon T3.

The T3 is a two-seater version of the Typhoon, an advanced fighter jet noted for its flexibility. With another pilot in place, Smith is able to focus his attention on mentally preparing for the rest of his mission. The T3 heads south toward Western Australia, with a necessary mid-flight refueling provided by an Airbus Voyager, the military version of the civilian Airbus A330.

The T3 lands at Royal Australian Air Force Base Pearce, which is about twenty miles north of Perth. As soon as the plane stops, a British Consulate Jaguar I-PACE, an all-electric SUV, pulls up next to the plane. Smith exits the plane and gets right into the SUV, which starts off immediately toward Perth International Airport.

A passenger plane at the airport has been boarded and is ready to depart for Washington DC. The plane's departure is delayed due to an official request by the Australian Secret Intelligence Service, which followed an urgent plea from MI6. Smith's vehicle drives up to a gate at the airport, whereupon Smith exits the Jaguar and gets into an official airport vehicle, which drives him to the delayed plane.

Smith boards the plane and apologizes humbly to the puzzled attendants and passengers, saying, "A thousand pardons, a thousand pardons."

One of the attendants, who is still flustered and wondering what kind of VIP he is, guides Smith to his seat in first class.

Smith says, "Many thanks." Before sitting down, he adds, "May I impose upon you for a drink?"

"What would you like?"

"A whiskey would do the trick nicely."

"One moment."

The attendant returns with his drink.

Smith graciously says, "Thank you kindly."

The plane is given priority for takeoff and it moves forward to the runway. After the plane takes off, Smith finishes his drink, pushes his seat back, and falls asleep immediately.

South China Sea

The ships and boats of the Chinese Navy are encircling Taiwan. Once in position, they begin to prevent any other ships or boats from entering or leaving Taiwan. Chinese Air Force planes begin patrolling the skies around Taiwan, preventing any other planes from arriving to or departing from Taiwan. The Chinese military is effectively blockading Taiwan.

The Chinese government releases a statement: "The government of the People's Republic of China has taken decisive action to prevent the outbreak in Chinese Taipei from spreading to the rest of the world. The People's Liberation Army has been ordered to prevent anyone or any traffic from entering or leaving Taiwan. This order will be carried out fully and decisively, including the use of whatever force might become necessary. All parties are directed to heed this announcement and to not interfere in any manner whatsoever with the implementation of the aforementioned order."

The government of Taiwan is already overwhelmed battling the virus outbreak, and the actions of the Chinese government push it to the breaking point. Taiwan is heavily dependent on imports for food, medical products, and oil, such that the blockade immensely exacerbates its already dire situation. Taiwan desperately reaches out for help, but no one responds. Taiwan is totally isolated and near collapse.

13

Washington DC

J ENNIFER IS DONNING her disguise again.

Suddenly, a communication pops up on Bobby's computer system: Aussie appears on the screen and announces, "Hey mate, I've got an update on that Yank Johnson."

Bobby responds, "What do you have?"

"I picked up some communications about him trying to bail on the feds in China, but that it did not go well for him."

"Thanks for the info."

"No worries. Catch you later."

Aussie disconnects.

Jennifer has been observing and says to Bobby, "Well, that makes it even more important to find out what's going on with Gates."

"It also seems to make it very clear how dangerous this whole situation is."

"I understood that when I saw what happened to Jim."

"I know. I just don't want the same thing to happen to you."

"I appreciate that. I'll be careful. I'm just planning to do some reconnaissance for now."

"Stay in contact with me. I have the area mapped out and will be monitoring you."

"Thanks, your help made all the difference last time."

Jennifer heads out, and Bobby monitors her as she walks down the street toward a Metro station. He uses the traffic camera network to watch her but loses the ability to monitor her after she heads onto the Metro. They planned for this, expecting the lack of video monitoring to last for about thirty to forty-five minutes. Bobby feels a bit apprehensive about not being able to see what's happening, but he uses the time to make sure he is fully prepared for when Jennifer exits the Metro. Finally, after what seems much longer to him than the actual forty minutes of elapsed time, Jennifer reappears on video.

"Hi, it's good to see you again."

"Hi. How is everything looking on your end?"

"It's looking fine; no problems."

Jennifer walks a few blocks down the street to a nondescript three-story building, with signage indicating that it is a Homeland Security building.

"I'm here. Can you see it?"

"Yes, I can see you and the building."

"There's a coffee shop across the street; it looks like a good location for observation of the building."

"Okay, I'll also observe and record, in case you want to review it later."

Jennifer goes into the coffee shop and is careful to pay in cash, which is a significant change for her after being so used to using a credit card for everything. She selects a seat with a good view of the Homeland Security building and begins the unexciting activity of observation. With the FBI, she had been involved in assisting with some stakeouts, so she knows the drill, including the general boredom of it. At least she finds the coffee to be tasty.

Several people come and go from the building; none of them seem very significant. Suddenly, a car pulls up next to the building, and the two men who had tried to bring Jennifer in just after James was killed get out of the car and enter the building. Jennifer feels very nervous and turns away for a moment to avoid being seen, but then she quickly turns back, as the logical part of her brain takes over again with the understanding that they won't be able to recognize her in disguise.

"Those two men are the ones who tried to take me in."

"Interesting. I have them on video."

"Great. Obviously, the loose ends seem to be coming together."

Smith's plane lands in Washington, and he is met at the airport by a representative from the British Consulate, who turns over a black four-door Land Rover Defender to him. Smith thanks him and then drives off, remembering to drive on the right side of the road. He activates the navigation and communications systems.

"Hi, mates, anything new?"

A male voice responds, "No. Your navigation is set up to take you to where they are holding Gates."

"Let me know if anything develops."

"Will do."

Smith arrives near the Homeland Security building. He parks down the street and walks toward the building, but on the opposite side of the street. Just as Jennifer did, he notices the coffee shop as being well located for observing the building and walks inside the shop. Being second nature to him in his job, he scans the coffee shop. Jennifer immediately stands out to him: she is in a seat ideally located for observing the building; she is looking directly at the building; she is talking but not into a phone; and she appears to be disguised.

Smith walks up to the counter, orders a black tea with lemon and pays for it.

"I'll have it ready for you in a moment," the counter server tells him.

Less than a minute later, the server hands the tea to Smith, who responds, "Thank you so much."

"You're welcome."

With a tilt of his head, Smith says, "Cheers," and he then walks over to where Jennifer is seated and asks, "May I sit here?"

Jennifer is caught off guard, having just been talking to Bobby, but especially given that the coffee shop is not very busy, with plenty of unoccupied areas for sitting. After an awkward pause, she finally says, "Sure, go right ahead."

"I'm new to the area. Do you have any recommendations for things to do?"

Jennifer is caught a bit off guard again; she is so focused on the building, and trying to figure out how all the pieces of the puzzle fit together, that she is not ready for a casual conversation. After another awkward pause, she responds, "There are lots of museums."

"You seem especially interested in that building across the street."

Jennifer is very surprised by Smith's comment and she gets up to leave, mumbling, "Not really. I have to go now."

Smith gets up also, and they both walk out of the shop. Jennifer's nervousness is rapidly increasing, and then she sees the two men she recognized earlier; they are now exiting the

Homeland Security building. Jennifer's natural reflex to turn away from the men to avoid being recognized takes over again; Smith notices this and comments, "You don't seem to want those blokes to see you."

Jennifer's blood pressure is soaring, and she tries to walk away from Smith.

Smith comments again, "They probably won't be able to recognize you in your disguise."

Jennifer is considering whether to try running away, but she quickly reviews the situation and figures that the two men who just walked out of the building would be tipped off if she did so, and that Smith seems to be in excellent shape to catch her; so instead, she blurts out, "Who are you, and what do you want?"

"I was wondering the same thing about you. I think we need to have a private conversation. I have a vehicle down the street."

Bobby has been listening and observing, and he says into Jennifer's ear, "Don't go with him. Get away now."

Jennifer continues her evaluation of the situation, which now includes a growing desire to know how this man is connected to the puzzle, and she decides to disregard Bobby's advice.

She says cautiously, "Okay."

They head down the street to Smith's vehicle. Once inside the Land Rover, Smith asks Jennifer which direction to take her, and he drives off that way.

Smith says, "How about if we get down to brass tacks? I'm thinking we are probably interested in the same thing, and there is really only one interesting thing about that Homeland Security building."

"Which is?"

"Dr. Gates."

Jennifer is surprised once again and responds, "What do you know about him?"

"Your turn," he replies. "What are you up to?"

Jennifer considers the various possibilities for the current situation before shrugging her shoulders and saying, "I'm with the FBI, and a friend of mine, who worked for the Secret Service, was killed shortly after getting back from a trip with the president to China. Now they are after me, and it seems as though Gates, and potentially gain of function research, might be connected to what happened to my friend."

"You're doing well. I just busted out an associate of Gates, Dr. Johnson, but the bad guys got him while he was making a break for it."

"We just heard about that."

J. E. STOCK

This time, Smith is surprised, as well as impressed. "How did you hear about it, and who are we?"

Bobby interjects in Jennifer's ear, "Don't tell him about me."

Smith notices Jennifer listening before she replies, "A friend of mine is helping me."

"A friend who would like to remain anonymous."

Jennifer smiles slightly and tilts her head in apparent agreement before asking, "And who are you?"

This time, Smith pauses for a moment before responding, "Well, as you've probably surmised, I'm a devious kind of guy, involved in all kinds of skullduggery."

"James Bond."

"The same group, essentially."

"So Bobby, what do you think? James Bond. Is it okay for me to bring him in?"

Bobby finally agrees with her, and Jennifer directs Smith to his place.

After they arrive and Smith sees Bobby's computer system, he looks around in amazement and comments, "Very impressive. You have your own personal GCHQ."

Bobby looks unsure for a moment, and Smith elaborates, "Government Communications Headquarters." Bobby then nods.

Introductions follow, and Bobby says, "Smith, I'm assuming, is an alias."

Smith replies, "It's easy to remember."

They all smile.

Then they get down to coordinating and planning. Smith introduces Bobby remotely to some of his MI6 associates assigned to the relatively new National Cyber Force, a joint effort between the Ministry of Defence and GCHQ, which just recently passed the five-year mark, and they coordinate on the computer side.

14

Washington DC

A S SMITH MAKES plans with Jennifer and Bobby, he receives a video communication through Bobby's computer system. Smith's supervisor appears and states, "We are running out of time. The Taiwanese government is collapsing, and an emergency special session of the UN General Assembly is going to begin debate a couple of hours from now, at ten o'clock, on a resolution to allow China to take over Taiwan in order to protect the rest of the world from the spread of the virus. A vote on the resolution is scheduled for four o'clock today. Following the UK's veto in the Security Council, China and the US have successfully worked together to move the issue to the General Assembly and to line up the votes, so you are our last hope. As you know, but for the benefit of your new friends, with Taiwan goes control of the South China Sea, which would allow China to totally dominate the area militarily and to control virtually all shipping through the region."

Smith responds, "Understood, we'll get started on our end."

He turns to Jennifer and Bobby and says, "As you heard, time seems to be running out. We'll have to charge ahead and improvise along the way, if necessary."

They both nod.

Jennifer and Smith get into his Land Rover, and he drives off. Bobby is monitoring them and asks, "Can you hear me okay?"

Jennifer replies, "Loud and clear."

While they are stopped at a traffic light, Smith says, "Open the glove box and help yourself."

Jennifer opens the glove compartment and sees two SIG Sauer P229 semiautomatic pistols. She takes one for herself and hands the other one to Smith.

He nods and asks, "Have you used one before?"

"Yes. My friend who was killed had one issued to him by the Secret Service, and I had a chance to try it out once when we were target shooting."

"Obviously, it's only for use when absolutely necessary."

"Totally understood."

"Let's not muck it up when we go in there. We want to go in and out quickly and smoothly."

"I get it; this isn't my first time at the rodeo."

They both smile.

"Check with Bobby."

"Bobby, is everything looking okay on your end?"

He replies, "Yes, we're all set. Everything is coordinated and in place."

She tells Smith, "He's ready."

Smith activates the communications system in the Land Rover and asks, "Are you ladies and chaps ready to go?"

A female voice responds, "Absolutely. Everyone is on their toes and ready for action."

"Brilliant, cheers."

About fifteen minutes later, Smith pulls over and parks near the Homeland Security building. He and Jennifer head into the building. Jennifer pulls out her FBI ID as they approach the security desk. She hands her ID to the officer managing the desk and asks, "Where is Gates being held?"

The officer shifts his attention away from Jennifer's ID for a moment, as he types on his computer, and then responds, "He's being held in room 211."

Bobby has been listening to the interaction between Jennifer and the security officer, and he passes along to his new partners from MI6, "It's time."

Someone from MI6 responds, "Righto, mate."

The security officer turns his attention back to Jennifer's ID; he's about to type into the computer again, when suddenly the system goes down. He taps hard on the keys, trying to get the system to respond. He then picks up his phone to call someone, but the phone is dead.

While the security officer is distracted, Smith casually drifts away toward a stairway. He then walks quickly up the stairway to the second floor and finds room 211. He knocks on the door.

A man opens the door and says, "Yes, what is it?"

Smith immediately hits him with a knockout blow and rushes into the room. Two other men are in the room, sitting at a table with Gates, and they head toward Smith. A rapid-fire series of blows, blocks, and counterblows takes place. Smith subdues the two men and then turns to Gates and says, "You're being rescued and it's time to leave."

Gates is totally startled, unsure of what is happening and what he should do. Smith impatiently grabs his arm and pulls him out of the room and to the stairway, where he says, "Down we go."

When they reach the bottom of the stairway, Gates asks, "Where are we going?"

This gets the attention of the security officer, who was still trying to figure out what was wrong with his computer and phone. He looks over and sees Smith and Gates coming from the stairway.

He reaches for his service revolver, but Jennifer draws her pistol and points it at him, commanding, "Hold it!"

The officer puts his hands up.

Smith and Gates come over to the security officer, and Smith says, "Turn around." After the officer turns around, Smith hits him on the back of the head, knocking him out.

Jennifer grabs her FBI ID, and they head out of the building, with Smith pulling Gates along. As they exit the building, they hear someone shout, "Hey you! Stop! What do you think you're doing?"

They turn and see two men crossing the street toward them. Jennifer exclaims, "It's the two guys who tried to take me in."

They run to Smith's Land Rover, with Smith still pulling Gates along, and get in just before the two men reach them. Smith locks the doors and starts the vehicle. The two men pound on the windows and then aim their guns at Smith. He hits the accelerator, and the vehicle lurches forward. The two men start shooting at them. Gates and Jennifer duck.

Smith says, "Don't worry, bulletproof is standard issue."

He then presses a button on the dashboard labeled MIRT, which stands for Mobile Infrared Transmitter. The device uses infrared LEDs to change traffic lights to green when approached.

The two men stop shooting at Smith's vehicle and run to their own vehicle. They jump in and give pursuit.

Bobby has been observing and coordinating with his MI6 partners. He says to them, "They won't last long like this. More feds are probably being called in right now."

An MI6 agent responds, "Agreed. They should have already activated the MIRT in their vehicle, but we need to do more to change the odds. Link us into the traffic camera system, and we will widen the coverage."

Bobby works on his computer for a few moments and then asks, "How's that?"

"Brilliant, mate; thanks. We'll use our team to monitor the incoming opposition."

Smith is intensely focused and drives at a high rate of speed, rapidly passing through intersections with the aid of his MIRT. Using his mirrors, he keeps an eye on the black SUV in pursuit. He suddenly accelerates, increasing the distance between them, such that a traffic light changes to red just a few seconds before the SUV, which does not have a MIRT, reaches the light. The opposing traffic has already started, and the driver of the SUV is forced to slam on the brakes and turn the vehicle sideways, but the momentum still carries them into the intersection, where they slam into another vehicle.

The driver of the SUV pounds his steering wheel and screams, "Damn it!" His partner uses the radio to alert others as to the location of Smith's vehicle and the direction it is heading.

Smith says sarcastically, "Back to driving school for him."

At their London headquarters, a group of several MI6 agents within the National Cyber Force are working on their computers in a coordinated effort to modify an algorithm in order to dynamically balance between the directional goal for Smith's vehicle and a maximization of the distance between Smith's vehicle and the pursuit vehicles. Then several of them comment almost simultaneously:

"Yes."

"That's it."

"We're ready to go."

An MI6 agent says to Smith through his vehicle's communications system, "Multiple vehicles are converging on you. Prepare for us to reroute you."

Smith responds, "Lead the way."

The MI6 algorithm is routed through the vehicle's navigation system, and the system's voice guides Smith through a series turns and other maneuvers to avoid the vehicles pursuing them.

The pursuit vehicles converge on the area where they expected to intercept Smith's vehicle. They stop and look around, confused and frustrated at finding no sign of them. A man gets out of the passenger side of one of the vehicles and looks around in all directions. He pounds his fist on the roof of the vehicle and then pulls out his cell phone.

He places a call and says, "We lost them."

After losing their pursuers, Smith slows down and turns off the MIRT, commenting, "It's time to blend in." He communicates to the MI6 team, "Good work, mates; it's greatly appreciated."

One member of the MI6 team responds, "Don't mention it."

In the backseat, Gates is in a state of panic. Unsure of who has rescued him, he is wondering if he should try to get out of the vehicle when it stops.

They stop at a red light, their first one in quite a while, thanks to the MIRT.

Jennifer comments, "I was really getting used to skipping these."

Smith responds, "I agree; civilian life seems to move in slow motion."

Gates, still unsure what to do, instinctively tries to open the door, mostly just to see if that option is available to him. He finds the door locked, and he is unable to unlock it.

Smith is observing him and comments, "It's called a child lock, but obviously it works for adults equally well."

Jennifer turns from the passenger seat to face Gates and smiles, saying, "Don't worry, Dr. Gates; we're on the same side." She pauses for a moment. "At least, I think we are."

Smith begins driving forward after the light turns green and interjects, "We are. The cavalry to the rescue, as you would say."

Gates asks, "Who are you?"

"I'm Smith, kind of on loan from British Intelligence to work with Agent Barnes here, who is with the FBI." Jennifer shows her ID to Gates.

"But what do you want with me?"

"You, Dr. Gates, are potentially the only one who can save the world from a highly dangerous change in the geopolitical balance of Southeast Asia."

"What do I have to do with Southeast Asia?"

"You sent Dr. Johnson to China to work on some rather dangerous viral gain of function research. The Chinese have taken over the work and weaponized it."

"Yes, I was on the phone with Johnson and heard them break into his apartment and arrest him. He did say that they took an extremely dangerous virus, just before the call was ended. I wasn't able to get through to him after that."

"We rescued him, just like we're doing with you, but your Chinese associates didn't want him to talk, so they shot down his plane."

"They wouldn't."

"Yes, they would, and they did. That leaves you. You might feel like a pawn in this global chess game, but you are really the king, who can win the game for the good guys."

"What can I do?"

"Obviously, Doctor, you can tell the world about the gain of function research that was being conducted in China and how the Chinese arrested Johnson and took the dangerous virus, which they have unleashed on Taiwan in order to be able to take over Taiwan and totally dominate Southeast Asia."

"No! Our research was intended to save lives, not take lives."

"You clearly didn't do quite enough due diligence on your partners."

"But why did Homeland Security arrest me and hold me in detention, rather than having me help expose what is going on?"

"Well, your president is a rather unsavory character. He did do his due diligence, and he chose to partner with the Chinese with, as you would say, his eyes wide open."

"That explains why he was so supportive of my avoiding the usual chain of command in order to do the research in China."

"And why you were arrested."

"Yes, I see now. So what is your plan?"

"We are going to take you to the United Nations to disclose what you know before the General Assembly votes to allow China to take over Taiwan, under the pretext of stopping the virus from spreading to the rest of the world."

"Well, if you can get me there, I will do everything I can to let them know what is really going on."

"Thank you, Doctor."

"I just feel so ashamed that I helped to make this tragedy possible. My goal in life has been to help people, not hurt them."

"I can't grant you salvation, but at least you are back with the good guys."

Jennifer interjects, "Yes, Doctor, focus for now on trying to rectify as much of the problem as possible."

Dr. Gates nods in agreement.

They gradually make their way out of the DC area.

The MI6 team is preparing for the next leg of Smith's journey, leveraging the UK's Space-Based Positioning, Navigation and Timing Programme (SBPP).

The team has been utilizing OneWeb, which provides broadband satellite internet service through its network of low-Earth orbit satellites, to communicate with Smith, but the satellites are too low to handle the needs of an advanced positioning, navigation, and timing (PNT) system. The UK government owns almost half of OneWeb, which it purchased when the company went bankrupt as a result of the COVID-19-related stock market sell-off, and it was hoped initially that it would also be able to handle the requirements for a PNT system. Additional work led to the conclusion that OneWeb would be unable to meet the needs of an advanced PNT system, which helped to spur the initiation of the SBPP.

The SBPP is still a work in process, but what has already been put in place provides an advanced and highly capable system. The National Cyber Force has top priority access to the system in place, including the right to redirect satellites, and they are fully ready to use this authority to assist in the next stage of the mission.

After leaving Washington, Smith drives north toward New York. He says to Jennifer and Dr. Gates, "Hopefully the two of you can rest a little now, after all of the excitement."

An MI6 agent communicates, "We are picking up increased security-related activity on your intended route. Prepare to be redirected."

"We're in your hands; go ahead."

Directions are once again passed along to Smith through the vehicle's navigation system, and he heads off on an alternate route. Even before the message regarding the need for a route change, Jennifer and Dr. Gates were too keyed up to rest, but that is especially the case now.

An MI6 agent communicates again, "A helicopter, which seems to be searching, is moving in your direction. You are one mile from a parking garage. We will direct you there."

Smith follows the directions to the parking garage.

After about fifteen minutes, the agent follows up, "It looks clear. Off you go."

Directions begin coming through again, and Smith heads out of the garage and gets back on the road.

He drives north for a couple of hours, and then the MI6 agent is back. "We have increased security activity ahead. This time, we're going to use a small off-road detour."

Smith follows the directions, leading to a rather bumpy ride for a few minutes. He apologizes, "Sorry for the rather uneven ride." He reaches a road again, ending the brief off-road adventure.

Smith drives for over an hour and is getting close to New York City when the MI6 agent says, "Security activity is heavy and increasing around New York. You are about five miles from the optional transfer location. We will direct you there."

"Got it."

A moment later the agent comes back on again, sounding concerned. "A helicopter is heading in your direction, and we don't have an option for you before the transfer location."

"We'll have to ride it out, then."

Smith tells Jennifer and Dr. Gates, "Hang on; this might get a bit hairy."

The helicopter heads toward them; through a loudspeaker, they are ordered to pull over. Smith ignores the request and speeds up instead. The helicopter moves lower toward their vehicle. The two men who tried to take Jennifer in are inside the helicopter with semiautomatic rifles. They begin to fire their weapons, repeatedly striking the roof of the vehicle.

Smith is driving extremely aggressively and weaving as much as possible. He says, "The armor plating should protect us."

Dr. Gates appears petrified.

The Land Rover is covered with a multitude of bullet impact locations, and there is still a continuous barrage of incoming bullets, but they are approaching the transfer location, which is a parking garage. Smith drives into the garage and finds a large van with an MI6 agent in the driver's seat, ready to go. The van pulls out of its parking spot, and Smith pulls in. They quickly transfer into the van and hide out of sight. The van then drives out of the garage and proceeds away from the helicopter hovering above.

About ten minutes later, security vehicles arrive at the garage and proceed inside, where they find the abandoned Land Rover.

In the helicopter, one of the men says, "They must be in that van that exited the garage."

The helicopter heads off in the direction the van was traveling. The van is exiting the Outerbridge Crossing into Staten Island when the helicopter reaches it. The helicopter hovers over the van for a couple of minutes and then uses its loudspeaker system to order the van to pull over. The van pulls over and the helicopter hovers lower to observe.

Suddenly, the back doors of the van open, and two motorcycles come out, the lead one driven by Smith and the next one driven by Jennifer, with Dr. Gates as an incredibly nervous passenger. The motorcycles rapidly accelerate, and the helicopter gives chase. The speeding motorcycles are weaving around and through the traffic and look like a blur to the other surprised drivers.

The MI6 team in London is discussing the situation, while Bobby listens in.

"The helicopter is chasing them."

"And how can they possibly get through New York and to the UN with the authorities alerted?"

Bobby interjects, "We need to take down the systems in New York and create some real chaos."

An MI6 agent responds, "We don't have the authority to do that; it could be considered an act of war. Temporarily taking out the power in a single building is one thing, but an attack on your biggest city is quite another, especially with your current president."

Another agent adds, "But we can't tell you what to do or not to do."

Bobby nods and says, "I understand."

He sends out a message: "Renegades, emergency, help needed ASAP."

The other Renegades check in immediately, and Bobby quickly lays out the situation: "We have a team on motorcycles that needs to run a gauntlet through the feds in New York to get to the UN in order to save Taiwan. We need to take down the systems in the city to create enough chaos for them to get through, while trying to not really hurt anyone."

The other Renegades respond:

"Wow, a real-life video game."

"I'm in, mate."

"Let's get started."

The Renegades all agree to help and begin working on the challenge.

The motorcycles are approaching the Verrazano Bridge to head into Brooklyn. They need to slow down a bit as they approach the bridge, and one of the men in the helicopter takes advantage of the reduced risk of collateral damage to other drivers to fire a few shots. One of the shots hits Smith in his left shoulder. He slumps for a moment, but keeps going, heading for the lower level of the bridge to get some cover from the helicopter. Jennifer follows right behind him. They weave through the traffic, generating a great deal of annoyance among the other drivers.

Some police vehicles are heading toward the Brooklyn side of the bridge to intercept the motorcycles. Smith hears the sirens and sees the vehicles heading on an intercept course for them. He speeds up and exits the bridge just as the police vehicles begin to reach the bridge, racing by them just before they have a chance to block the road, with Jennifer right behind and Dr. Gates holding on for dear life.

The Renegades are struggling with their challenge. One of them says, "We need more help."

Bobby understands and responds, "I will get on it immediately."

He sends out a message: "Hackers Unite for Freedom! The Renegades have an urgent real-life challenge to help a team with secret information to save Taiwan pass through New York to reach the UN. They are in immediate danger of being arrested, and we need to create enough chaos to help them get through."

Smith leads the way north through western Brooklyn, but police vehicles are converging on the area. He hears the sirens and sees some of the vehicles moving to block their path, but it also appears that the police are moving to push them toward the Upper Bay, in order to box them in. Smith slows down, turns right, and begins backtracking somewhat, heading southeast. Jennifer follows close behind. After diverting away from where the police are heading, Smith then turns back and heads northwest.

The Renegades are making some progress, but they are still struggling to do enough to really accomplish their goal. One of them comments, "We're not getting any significant help."

Bobby responds, "I know. Let's continue to do as much as we can."

Smith avoids additional police vehicles heading west, as he heads toward the Brooklyn Bridge. Then the helicopter that attacked them previously reappears above them. Smith notices it and accelerates.

The Renegades are working feverishly, when they suddenly notice help arriving. They see comments appearing, including "Long live Taiwan" and "Freedom for Taiwan." One of the Renegades exclaims, "It's the Taiwanese."

The Renegades continue their work with a renewed fervor, spurred on by their newly gained support.

Smith is approaching the Brooklyn Bridge and sees police vehicles heading toward the bridge on the Manhattan side. He drives onto the pedestrian and bike portion of the bridge, in order to avoid the congested vehicle lanes, as he races to beat the police. He and Jennifer speed across the bridge, with pedestrians jumping out of the way. They exit the bridge and head past the arriving police cars, which are swerving to try to stop them.

Traffic lights suddenly start going out of control; some lights go all green and others go all red. Access has been gained to some traffic light controllers and malfunction management units, as well as some conflict monitor units.

Power is lost in some areas. Elevators in many office buildings stop functioning. The subway system is forced into a shutdown.

People begin to pour onto the streets, adding to the congestion. Traffic, throughout the city, plunges into total chaos.

The police are overwhelmed.

The Renegades are ecstatic.

"It's working!"

"We did it!"

"This is incredible!"

Smith heads north through Manhattan, with Jennifer right behind and Dr. Gates still managing to hold on. They weave through the traffic jams and pedestrians, while the police struggle to deal with the chaos. The helicopter flying above breaks off and heads north.

They are approaching midtown. Smith has lost a lot of blood from the bullet wound to his shoulder, but his tenacity and training drive him on to complete his mission. They continue to maneuver through the chaotic environment, closing in on their goal.

They pull up in front of the United Nations complex, get off their motorcycles, and head to the General Assembly building. As they approach the entrance, shots ring out. One shot hits Smith in his right leg, causing him to dip down slightly, and another grazes Jennifer's left arm. The shots were fired by the two men who've been pursuing them. Smith and Jennifer both swing around while pulling out their pistols and then fire at the men, each hitting one of them. They turn back around and head into the building, with Dr. Gates asking them if they are okay. They both nod.

An aide to the UK ambassador greets them in the lobby, and has them discreetly discard their weapons in a trash can. He escorts them through security, where their wounds generate some interest from the security personnel, but he waves them off. Then they quickly head to the Assembly Hall, where the General Assembly is meeting. As they are seen, after entering the Hall, with their multiple bleeding wounds, there are many gasps and a general state of shock. The current speaker stops mid-sentence and just stares at them.

When they reach the UK ambassador, he talks to them briefly and then announces loudly, "Mr. President, we have critical evidence to be presented."

The Chinese and US ambassadors try to object, but the UK ambassador waves them off, saying, "You have had your opportunity, and now it is our turn. Please go ahead, Dr. Gates."

Dr. Gates steps up and begins, "My name is Dr. Michael Gates, and I am the director of the US National Institute of Allergy and Infectious Diseases. I made the mistake of engaging in dangerous viral gain of function research with the government of the People's Republic of China. I did so over the objections of my supervisor, but with the approval and support of the president of the United States. The PRC subsequently commandeered a dangerous virus which was created through this research and then, against any reasonable basis for civilized human behavior, engaged in biological warfare by introducing the virus to Taiwan. During this process, they arrested and then later killed a colleague of mine who was involved in the research and found out what the PRC was doing."

There is general astonishment among the ambassadors. The Chinese ambassador begins to object, but seeing the disdain from the other ambassadors, he just walks out instead.

A vote on the resolution is taken, and it is overwhelmingly defeated.

The UK ambassador turns to Smith, Jennifer, and Dr. Gates and thanks them. He then says to his aide, "Get some medical attention immediately for these heroes."

CPSIA information can be obtained
at www.ICGtesting.com
Printed in the USA
LVHW030256240821
695968LV00004B/141

9 781664 178984